A Little Girl Under a Mosquito Net

A Little Girl Under a Mosquito Net

by Monique Lange

Translated from the French
by Patsy Southgate

A Richard Seaver Book

The Viking Press
New York

For Frédéric

First published by Editions Gallimard in Paris, France,
under the title *Une petite fille sous une moustiquaire*
© Editions Gallimard, 1972
English-language translation Copyright © 1973 by
The Viking Press, Inc.
All rights reserved
A Richard Seaver Book | The Viking Press
Published in 1973 by The Viking Press, Inc.
625 Madison Avenue, New York, N.Y. 10022
SBN 670-43193-1
Library of Congress catalog card number: 73-6085
Printed in U.S.A.

Rejoice with me; for I have found
my sheep which was lost.

—GOSPEL ACCORDING TO SAINT LUKE

Religion is the opium of the people.

—KARL MARX

Darling takes the photo, puts it on his
tongue, and swallows it.

"I adore your Lady of the Flowers,
I take her in Holy Communion."

—JEAN GENET, *Our Lady of the Flowers*

Childhood

AS OTHERS are tempted by the Devil, so I was tempted by God. Even as a little girl, probably because my family was serenely atheistic, I wanted to have a God. At first the Jewish God, but he terrified me. He stood only for anger, destruction, vengeance, and I wanted a God of love, I wanted love. Christ fascinated me all the more because he was forbidden, and I started collecting little aluminum medals, holy pictures, rosary beads, all of this on the sly because while my family was not orthodox, it was sincerely Jewish.

At school, all my classmates took first communion, but in our faith, only boys had that privilege. This primordial discrimination offended me. There were male rabbis, but no female rabbis, only rabbis' wives—yet there were priests and nuns, Jesuits and Carmelites—and besides, with the non-Jews, love was everything while with us everything was thunder, flood, chastisement, expiation, and I already had a wild need to be loved.

I *was* loved, however. By an adorable grandmother who raised me after my parents' divorce when I was three years old.

We lived in Paris in large apartments, first on avenue Malakoff—my birthplace—at the bottom of the old Trocadero, then on rue de l'Assomption where I experienced my first religious temptations, and finally on rue de Marignan which I left for Saigon in 1939, a few months before war was declared.

One of my first mystical memories is linked to fear. On rue de l'Assomption I was afraid to cross the hall to go to the bathroom; I would pace around in my room and, when I couldn't stand it any longer, I would urinate on the brown carpet. Then I would move an armchair over to hide my heinous crime and fall to my knees at the other end of the room to beg for pardon. Already—I must have been five or six—the Virgin or Saint Francis of

Assisi seemed more tolerant to me than the Jewish God.

What displeased me the most about the Jewish religion was that God did not want images to be made of Him. And I wanted to see Him. It didn't make sense. All my Catholic friends had gorgeous crucifixes hanging above their beds, pictures of another mother: the Blessed Virgin, and reassuring golden medals, while all I had was a little *chadail* (a heart with a few Hebrew words written on it), and besides, Hebrew was a harsh-sounding language, and Latin was what we were taught in school.

We spent the last part of our vacation in Chaubuisson—near Fontenay-Trésigny—on a big estate which later became a hotel, and we played in the forest. We played at praying, praying for entire afternoons, our knees all pitted by the tiny pebbles. I softly said my rosary, pink and blue, crystalline, transparent. I kissed the little carved beads. I learned Our Father, Hail Mary, and the confiteor in delicious secrecy.

Pierrot and Gigi were going to get married in the church at Fontenay-Trésigny. Pierrot was an exemplary boy. He worked in the beet factory in Coulommiers and, every Sunday, bicycled twenty-five miles to see Gigi, his fiancée. Twenty-five miles on a bicycle, that was real love. If Papa had bicycled twenty-five miles every Sunday, my parents never would have got divorced. I hung around for hours in that church, praying for a faithful Catholic husband, a husband who would bicycle to the ends of the earth for me. We made cider, too. It was September. It was my birthday. I drank too much of it. I got sick to my stomach. It wasn't serious. God would heal me. He had chosen me. I was having a love affair with God. I had been elected. Papa was a candidate for deputy. He was not elected. You had to pray to be elected. You had to mortify your flesh like the decomposing apples. You had to ferment. I already loved the rotten smell before the grape harvest. You had to deserve the wine.

I entered the church. The incense, the little lights, the miracles. Everything smelled sweet. The candles were burning brightly. You knelt down. The altar was the outer limit of the earth. A white tablecloth for eating God. A lace cloth. A coat of gold as heavy as sin. The music. The confessional. The nave. The grille. Prison of love where you prostrated yourself to take communion. Sticking out your tongue to God. I am not worthy to receive you. I loved the smell of the church. The stone. The incense. The slight odor of rot. Perhaps that's why they say a "stinking nun."

I had a Swedish governess. Cruel. Virtuous. Protestant. I begged her to let me go inside churches. It amused her to see me betray the Jewish God and, since she was the first to know that I had acquired a taste for contrition, she pinched me until she drew blood if I hadn't learned my lessons properly.

"What on earth happened to you?" my luminous grandmother asked.

"I bumped into something," answered the bad seed of Christian that I was.

"I don't know what's the matter with that girl. Tell us what's bothering you."

I knew that I must say nothing. Pontius Pilate handed over Jesus. I would keep still. *Before the cock crow, thou shalt deny me thrice.*

In the country, the cock's crowing was linked for me to Christ's Passion. Oh how I loved that word! How voluptuously excessive it was. Everything in the gospel seemed so accessible to me: the cocks, the grass, the tares, the pearls, the nets, the thorns, the little loaves of bread like Charlie Chaplin's, the water changed into wine, the first stones. Only the Resurrection worried me. There would be too many of us up there, surely.

To leave Paris was to find God. He lived in the grass, in the hay, in the forest. His sweet smell came from lilies of the valley, and the moss at the feet of the oak trees looked like the fuzzy green hair of little black angels.

The trees in Paris were prisoners of the houses, and the houses were prisoners of the trees. In Paris, the churches did not breathe, neither did the schools. In Paris, God stopped for red lights.

In Fontenay-Trésigny, there were bushes where we picked blackberries and lilacs in the garden which was redolent of wisdom.

Behind the bushes with my little friends, I would crush geranium petals against my lips. Why shouldn't Christ's fiancée have red lips?

God was everywhere. I had found him. He had to accept me. I began to stroke everything that came to hand. "She's always pawing everything, that child!" Velvet, satin, the texture of the walls, tree bark, mud, marble, porcelain, grass, hair. I stroked the eggs as they emerged all warm from the hen house and sucked them. Was it God I was swallowing? God was everywhere.

I was an intrepid little girl who pawed everything. The discovery of faith taught me the meaning of sin, but before that I had no qualms whatever about taking down my pants in front of my two boy cousins and showing them what I didn't have so that they would show me their little bird. We played doctor, and Papa and Mama, and school, under the embroidered tablecloths, in the coat room, near the front door on rue de Marignan, and in the barns. My sense of sin was tied to these hiding places until virtue gripped me at puberty, but at ten I was utterly bold and innocent.

One of my boy cousins was entrancing-looking but quite a sissy. He was more feminine than I, and prettier. He was the one people would turn around to look at in the street and say, "Oh, what a lovely little girl!" He was the one who got chosen for the Bébé Cadum poster. I wasn't really jealous of all this, but I did want to give him his comeuppance. I adored giving people their comeuppances.

One day, eavesdropping on a grownups' conversation, I overheard a discussion about a difficult delivery one of our aunts had gone through: "She suffered tortures. They had to give her a Caesarean."

A Caesarean, that was like an Arlésienne or a julienne (either a piece of music or a soup that they had put in her stomach). I couldn't breathe a word of this. Ever. They must never know I knew about it.

But I told the whole story of the delivery to my pretty cousin as though it had been a terrible siege: babies came out through your bellybutton, boys gave birth to boys and girls to girls, and it hurt so much that you never wanted to go through it again, and that's why we were only children.

I hated being an only child. It meant being alone. I was lonely. I did everything I could to try and make myself interesting. When I went skating at Molitor, I fell down so someone would have to pick me up. I fished for pity. I fished for love. I was like little Trott of Lichtenberger who used to throw himself out of his chair to see if his parents loved him.

I loved clowns, beggars, brides and grooms, florists, and shepherds. I loved everything that made me cry.

On Thursday afternoons and Sunday mornings, I used to go to the stamp market with my cousin Yves. It was near rue de Marignan, on avenue Gabriel.

On the top shelf of the bookcase, which was in the hall on rue de Marignan, I had come upon the stamp collection which had belonged to my great-uncle, my grandmother's brother who had died in the First World War and whose portrait, along with his *Croix de guerre,* was enshrined on Grandmama's mantel, next to the worn little radio that rattled off stock-market prices from the Bourse. I used to believe that he was the Unknown Soldier, but that didn't stop me from tearing stamps, one by one, out of his album and reselling or exchanging them in front of my astonished cousin, who hardly dared ask who had given them to me. I would say airily, "A man." I was already a thief and a sinner and overwhelmed with remorse. I asked God's pardon for fleecing a soldier who had died on the field of honor. Then, when I thought I had been forgiven, I would climb up on the bookcase again and unglue three or four more stamps, which I would hide, radiant, feverish, under my pillow: beautiful red, mauve, or blue crowned heads. Sometimes I would climb up one more time and steal a Hindenburg, a lady sowing wheat, a king of Thailand.

It was the summer of 1932. We were in Socoa —opposite Saint-Jean-de-Luz—at the Dreyfusses', first cousins of my grandmother who came to a tragic end. They were on board the steamship *George-Philipart* when it burned off Alexandria in 1933. Rescued almost miraculously, they perished in the plane that was bringing them back to Paris.

That was the first time I heard the word "destiny" spoken. But that summer, the whole family was gathered together. I adored Paul Dreyfuss, who was a thoroughly charming adventurer. I showed him a petal of a white flower which had a little yellow pollen on it, and said, "Look, Paul, it looks like a fried egg." He exclaimed, "This little girl is going to be a poet," or something like that. I latched on to that idea. I was proud, happy, I was going to be famous. I launched into absurd comparisons—for example, that I was the shepherdess of the sheep of the sea.

I talked baby talk to my Raynal dolls. I swore to them that I would never get divorced, never go out at night, and always take them with me on my vacations.

Jesus cast the money-changers out of the temple, but I didn't know that yet. At night, before going to sleep, I would wrap all my childish treasures in toilet paper, my chain, my *chadail,* my little watch, and my grandmother's cuff links, and barter them back and forth underneath the bolster.

We were exercising in the courtyard of the Victor-Duruy school.
I was ten years old and hated gymnastics.

I noticed that when the older girls said, "I don't feel well," they were excused: that must be a good gimmick.

As flat-chested as a little Breton sole, I said to the teacher, "Madame, I don't feel well, may I . . ."

"Already, my child?"

She sent me to the infirmary. They gave me two aspirins, but the second time I didn't get away with it.

That same year, Madamoiselle Marc, our math teacher, scolded me because I didn't even begin to understand one of the problems. I burst into tears: I would *never* understand math! She said, "Save your tears for your tragic love affairs."

That remark sent me up into the clouds. Tragedy? Love? The magic number of tears was love. I might never know anything about mathematics, but I would understand love.

I focused my myth of man on a few very hairy grownups. At the Voza pass, there was a handsome instructor named Muckenbrunn. He taught skiing dressed in a sumptuous navy-blue angora sweater that quivered in the snow like the tendrils on Marlene Dietrich's feather dress which Professor Unrat blew on slavishly on a postcard of *The Blue Angel*.

The members of my family were subject to terrible migraine headaches. My uncle's vision would blur, and once my grandmother, landing in Venice, had such a violent attack that she failed to see the gangplank and fell into the water.

Images like these were in my head as a child, like the reverse of Botticelli's Venus rising from the sea. My grandmother was divine, and her fall into a Venetian canal was an almost religious image— perhaps the ritual immersion, the wrongheaded baptism that I would later reject.

While they didn't take much care of my soul when I was a little girl, at least they did take care of my body. I went to rhythm classes with Irene Popard and gymnastics with Dimitri Kandaouroff at 9, rue Anatole-de-la-Forge, right near the Étoile.

One, two, three, one, two, three. They were Russian émigrés. I adored them and acquired at their sides a passion for foreign accents that would never leave me.

After gymnastics, the old lady would stuff me with cheese tarts and tea. I gorged myself. That was the beginning of my fleshly inconsistencies.

And she told me their story: Her husband had had a very important post in Moscow and traveled through Russia on a private train. Then the Revolution broke out and they wound up on one of the Prince's Islands, opposite Constantinople, with their two sons. What she remembered about it was the odor of wisteria and the immensity of the blue sky when they slept in the Turkish fields.

At the Rond-Point des Champs-Élysées, we used to go to the puppet show, and I would hide in the bushes.

A little girl with a future in Charles Swann's arms, I voluptuously ate my pistachio ice cream in its crunchy cone. I pushed the ice cream way into the bottom of the cone with my tongue and pretended delight at the ice-cream man's loving me madly and filling my cone down to the very bottom.

At the Pré-Catelan, I always begged them to sprinkle lots of white powder on my warm waffles.

We were eating dinner on rue de l'Assomption. My uncle/my idol had had an automobile accident. He had gone to sleep at the wheel of his car and run into a wall. They telephoned us from the country.

My grandmother sprang to her feet, rent with anguish. Protected, sheltered little girl that I was, I discovered with a jolt that young and handsome people could die. My grandmother left at once.

When I got back into my brown room, I prayed: "My God, let that wall be soft, my God, let that wall be made of cotton, my God, don't let him die."

My prayer was granted. My uncle did not die. I vowed never to pee on the carpet again. I saw him afterward at Épinal, young, mysterious with his white golf balls that looked as though they had the chicken pox and those tees (little wooden nails before plastic was invented) on which you rested the ball. I mixed the tees in with my rosary beads, in order to pray better. On Sunday, when he came to see us, we ate meringues with whipped cream, but what he liked best were tarts made out of red fruit (plums, cherries, strawberries, raspberries).

He was the grownup of my dreams. I loved grownups. One day I would be a grownup and then I would be loved.

We almost always spent the month of September with our great-grandmother in Toulouse (the strange longevity of the women in my family, a longevity cut short in my grandmother's and my mother's cases).

Near the Place Wilson where we lived in Toulouse there was a pink candy-store owner, a friend of the family's, who delighted me with his big smile that seemed to say, "I won't eat you up, my child." We called him Chocolat. I loved going into that

candy store where the saleswomen, as old as the
candy dynasty they represented, spoiled me. They
looked so happy. I had a sugary vision of happiness.
I always left with some chocolates in a little porcelain basket tied with a pink bow. Sometimes also
with sugar Parma violets or mimosas which melted
on my tongue like the white communion wafers that
were forbidden to me. The chocolates my grandfather liked best had white cream fillings. You could
get them at Sirdar's, on the Avenue des Champs-
Élysées, where we always went after our trip to the
movies on Sunday morning.

That Sunday-morning picture show was my Jewish mass. There were cartoons, Charlie Chaplin
movies, Buster Keaton, and newsreels.
During the newsreels I was always frightened by
something or someone, whereas Charlie Chaplin
made me cry deliciously as I held on tightly to my
grandfather's hand. I was afraid of the Japanese:
Mama was in Indochina; I was afraid of the Germans: they were the traditional enemy. The man I
really liked because he looked peaceful, as though
he wouldn't hurt a fly, was President Albert Lebrun.

I had a passion for Negus, and I detested Musso-
lini who was hurting him. I was also convinced that
politics led inevitably to war. That's why I didn't

want my father to be a candidate for deputy from the Dreux region, where he sometimes took me on Sunday.

However, the opposition posters reassured me. They read: *Robert Lange, candidate defending the* mérite agricole, *can he tell a cabbage from a beet?*

Before going to bed, my grandfather would empty his pockets onto a Louis XV dresser with a white marble top that I adored resting my cheeks or forehead on. Sometimes, while he was shaving, I would snitch one or two of his one-franc pieces. My generous and disorderly grandfather would never notice.

One day, however, I couldn't resist, and I snitched six or seven, and heard him ask my grandmother, "Don't you sometimes have the impression that Jeanne, the chambermaid, is going through my pockets?"

"You're dreaming," answered my charming grandmother.

And so I was deprived of my punishment. God did not have the answer for trifles such as these.

I read the *Fables* of La Fontaine and Perrault's *Fairy Tales.*

Blue Beard drove me crazy, but for mysterious reasons. Not because he was ugly, not because of the sin of curiosity, but because I didn't have any broth-

ers who might have rescued me from my execu-
tioner. I would therefore be punished for something
I had not done. There was no possible savior for me,
I had only God to turn to.

And in the awful porridge they made me choke
down every morning, it was His name I wrote with
my spoon as the two pieces of butter melted sadly in
the bowl at the bottom of which three little pink
roly-poly pigs awaited me.

Mama remarried when I was nine. I wasn't sad
because it was delightful being raised by
grandparents—and besides, her marriage meant
going on a long voyage. Japan, Indochina, sun-filled
photographs, palm trees, junks, pineapples.

She wrote to us every week, and described her life
in terms of mangoes, tortoise-shell bracelets, bou-
gainvillaea, three servants, a convertible Juva, recep-
tions where the lobsters had little lights in their
eyes, swimming pools, ice-cold drinks, and "here
everything is dirt cheap." In short, a life of ease, of
light. "How soft Mama's colonies were."

For my tenth birthday, in 1936, I went to visist
her with my grandmother and her new husband's
sister.

In 1936, as it looked from the rue de Marignan,
the workers were "running amuck"; rioting on Place

de la Concorde, and the son of friends of the family
was wounded by them and had to go about in a little wagon for the rest of his life.

In the family cotton mill, lost by my uncle in a
gambling game, they were paternalistic. The workers had given my uncle/my idol a silver-plated sheaf
of wheat for his twentieth birthday.

He was handsome, young, divorced. It seemed to
me that he had a lot of mistresses. A mistress was a
woman who cheated on her husband, and therefore
was a wicked woman. How could he resist wicked
women? Whores were nicer, because they were poor,
and they never had husbands.

I was proud, vaguely proud of my uncle's mistresses. The only thing I feared was that he might
get hurt.

He was Monsieur André, we were Mademoiselle
Monique and Monsieur Yves, but we addressed the
gardener and the cook as Julien and Anna.

We spent our vacations in a big house in Épinal,
in the Vosges. There were porcelain roosters and
copper pots in the kitchen. Anna made pumpkin
soup and whortleberry jam for us. Sitting on the
banks of the Moselle, we ate mints while reading
The Adventures of Bicot and listened to our pam-
pered childhood gurgle by like water.

Julien had to have a prostate operation. He was
Anna's husband. Who would pick the gooseberries?

Who would water the dahlias? Who would fix the swing? There was whispering inside the house. The prostate must be an illness of the poor, like the Popular Front.

The family mill was called Kahn & Lang Manuel. Manuel was my grandparents' name. I always wondered who that Monsieur Cananlang was and why we never saw him.

Indochina

MAMA WANTED us to see her happiness for ourselves. That happiness was made of frangipani, royal poincianas, the temples of Angkor, white rice, cane sugar, shantung dresses that rustled at the touch, China tea, green-jade bracelets that you held against your temples to chase away Western migraine headaches, and gold pendants with characters, indecipherable to us, which meant Felicity, Fatherland, or Eternity.

Their house was completely white and surrounded by a large garden. Perhaps the garden was small, but my desire to have them be happy was so strong that I saw everything, from the height of my ten years, as large and harmonious: my mother's laugh was a waterfall, their love was what love was meant to be, her tiny hands were flowers, and when they showed us skeletons in anatomy class at school, I could see every woman as one except her.

My stepfather worked for the Franco-Asiatic Petroleum Company. The *bep* (cook) made us wonderful surprise omelets. We learned how to eat with chopsticks. The sky was blue. It was very hot. We left the house and shouted, *"Keo, Keo,"* to the rickshaw coolies who fell all over themselves to take us on our silken errands.

I, who could already be moved to tears by clowns and beggars, still wonder how on earth I found it natural for those skinny men to be hauling us around as though they were beasts of burden. My stepfather, who was a "liberal," wrote this to me ten years later:

The French people want to treat the Vietnamese as equals. You know them, and you know that this is impossible. From a physical point of view, they are different from us. That is a fact, and it cannot be helped. From an intellectual point of view, it is the same story. . . .

In the Saigon house there was a mysterious room with a platform in it: a wooden bed with hard little cushions to rest your head on. That was where they went for their "siesta."

My mother was a fairy. She had bewitched the wood with her magic wand. She had invented a country where one slept alive on planks. Next to the platform, there were long pieces of wood like flutes, and an odor like incense drifted through the room —sandalwood, jasmine, rose, poppy, yellow lily. I had already smelled these musky odors at the Colonial Exhibition and in my beloved churches.

I harbored a sweet-smelling nostalgia for that first trip to Indochina. France could not hold a candle to our perfumed colonies. Only my grandmother could be the makeweight, tender, adored. And yet one night in February, when I was sleeping soundly the way children do, I awoke with a start.

Tap. Tap. Tap. Three little knocks on the wall. My grandmother was calling me. Just before she died, she asked me to burn her account books so that her mother, my great-grandmother, would never know the foolish amounts she had spent on my grandfather up until her very last days.

She had large sea-green eyes, and an infinite gentleness. She placed herself in the background out of love. My grandfather was unfaithful to her. He was the only man she ever loved.

The last image I have of her: She was walking with a large suitcase containing fabrics by Madeleine Vionnet. She was working as a "representative," undoubtedly to provide pocket money for my grandfather.

Tap. Tap. Tap. My grandmother, wonder of wonders.
My grandmother died that morning.
Would that be the end of my childhood?
I was thirteen.
"We'll send her to live with her mother in Saigon."
Saigon, what bliss! How sweet it was that death always engendered something new.

For a child, a death is a celebration. You lose someone only to find someone else. One mother would replace the other. I still have a photograph of those delightful vacations in Knokke-Le Zoute with my grandmother, where we looked so happy. She adored me. Her children had grown up by then and all had gotten divorced. She wrapped me in the bunting from the lost cotton mill. It was a time when people really protected children from the world. I didn't know *anything*. Poverty reached me through Andersen's *Fairy Tales,* trouble through Perrault's *Fairy Tales,* and God from heaven knows where.

On rue de Marignan, on my great-grandmother's night table, there was a book of prayers in Hebrew that I used to leaf through before lunch while she listened to the stock prices from the Bourse.

"What good things are we having to eat today, Marie?"

"Cauliflower au gratin, Madame, and beautiful little steaks."

Baruch Adonai—Rhône-Poulenc—Hammevoror —Péchiney—Leolom Voed—Kali-Sainte-Thérèse and Royal Dutch pray for us.

For our great-grandmother, widowed at forty, nothing was more sacred than the family.

She looked after everything for us the way she wanted us to look after ourselves.

"How tragic! How tragic!" she moaned, wringing her hands: my grandmother was her daughter.

Then:

"You must be a very good little girl, very well-behaved."

"Yes, Great-grandma."

"There, come and give me a kiss, you're a brave little girl."

Of course I was brave! I was going to cross the Mediterranean, the Red Sea, the Indian Ocean and rejoin my dear mama and her brand-new husband from the Far East. I adored those words which meant that there would always be something special about my family.

Just as some people are intensely colorful, so certain Jewish widows, heavy in their astrakhan coats, are intensely black. Our great-grandmother, widowed at forty, eternally faithful to that husband who had left a Tilbury carriage on her doorstep along with his marriage proposal, was intensely black.

She had spent her life adoring her children, playing bridge every afternoon, and going on cruises with another old lady, a fashionable antique dealer, Madame Doucet.

Her passion for travel had also led her to buy several shares of stock in Russian railways and the Tramways of Shanghai, and when someone asked, after her world tour, "Is Cyprus beautiful, my dear Hermance?"

She answered, "I got a grand slam on Cyprus, a slam in spades."

And I wondered if the Grand Slam was a Cypriot Sultan whom my great-grandmother had rapped with her fan like the Dey of Algiers who had struck the wicked consul with his fly swatter.

For this second trip to Indochina, this second trip for grandmother's little orphan, this second trip which would take me back to my mama, my uncle/my idol accompanied me to Marseille and handed me over to a couple of clerks from Quinon, the Savary-Ricordeaux, who were charged with looking after me during our month at sea, and then with turning me over to my mother.

My grandmother's best friend gave me—along with thirty little presents, one to open each day of the trip—a package of white cotton "in case something happens to you on the ship."

"When you see me again, I'll be a woman," I had told my father.

"Above all, don't be scared," she told me. "It's perfectly normal. You're almost a young lady now."

Without this blood, I knew that I would not exist. But I was afraid of that blood, afraid of it as of a second birth and, as a result, I was afraid of crossing the Red Sea, although I had already ascertained that it was not red. Grownups' lies, when would they stop tormenting me? But since it had all worked out for Moses, why wouldn't it work out for me?

It had worked out. But at what a price. Why did God have to be on one side and not the other?

The engulfment of the Egyptians struck me as being a terrible injustice. Why them and not us?

"The Jewish God has never been a vengeful God," my great-grandmother used to say. Quite the contrary, since the Jewish people were chosen by God, who saved them from slavery to the Egyptians.

And during our first stopover in Cairo, perched on a camel led by a little Arab, contemplating the dazzling Pyramids, I wondered why God had chosen the Jews, what that really meant, and in an agony read and reread page 61 of my vengeful Bible:

. . . and the waters were divided. And the children of Israel went into the midst of the sea upon the dry ground: and the waters were a wall unto them on their right hand and on their left. . . . And the Egyptians pursued, and went in after them to the midst of the sea, even all Pharaoh's horses, his chariots and his horsemen. And it came to pass that in the morning watch the Lord looked unto the host of the Egyptians through the pillar of fire and of the cloud, and troubled the host of the Egyptians, and took off their chariot wheels, that they drove them heavily: so that the Egyptians said, "Let us flee from the face of Israel; for the Lord fighteth for them and against the Egyptians." And the Lord said unto Moses, "Stretch out thine hand over the sea, that the waters may come again upon the Egyptians, upon their chariots, and upon their horsemen." And Moses stretched forth his hand over the sea, and the sea returned to his strength when the morning appeared; and the Egyptians fled against it; and the Lord overthrew the Egyptians in the midst of the sea. And the waters returned, and covered the chariots, and the horsemen and all the host of Pharaoh that came into the sea after them; there remained not so much as one of them. . . . And Israel saw the Egyptians dead upon the seashore. . . .

Everything went smoothly on board ship. I didn't like the Savary-Ricordeaux very much but I liked the sailors a lot, the steward, and the officer who operated the radio and collected blue butterflies.

The officer who had the blue butterflies was the one who kept us in contact with the world. He picked up distress signals from sinking ships, S O S's.

In his cabin, there was a photograph of his wife and children. He was at home about three months out of the year. I wondered if his wife was unfaithful to him as in the songs.

One day I got a spanking from the clerk or his wife because I'd been found in the hold sitting on a sailor's lap. And yet I was still utterly innocent and completely naïve, and would clasp the pillow against me in my cabin, at night, troubled by feelings I couldn't identify.

I remember our ports of call: Djibouti: flies. Ceylon: curry. Singapore: Hindu merchants. Everywhere a mixture of beggars, poverty, bloated bellies, and trachoma, of soldiers and shopkeepers. But to the little girl that I was then, the world seemed to be established in this mixture of injustice and misery as though irrevocably.

I can't really remember our arrival in Saigon or the delivery by the Savary-Ricordeaux of the little-girl-package from rue de Marignan who was to become the little-girl-package from rue Garcerie.

In the apartment on rue Garcerie—my parents had moved, they no longer lived in the fragrant frangipani-filled house of 1936 but on a long passageway that looked out on some trees—I had a room with a double bed in it. Above the bed an immense white mosquito net presided over all my dreams about marriage in a cathedral.

I did not forget the obstacle of my birth. I placed it between parentheses as between a pair of cherubs, already dreaming of a possible redemption.

Like Napoleon and Josephine (she was dark, pagan, damned), he would place a crown of roses on my head. Tea roses from China. A cathedral. Lilies. A white tulle veil. Incense. Jasmine. The altar boy would swing a golden basket full of troubling odors over our heads. I recognized the chalice: it was the cup my uncle had won at golf, and the host: Grandmama's Kalmine tablets. God was in His heaven.

The thing about Christians was that they knew more about magic. I would marry a magician. I would be the widow in black of a man who had never loved anyone but me. I would be a bishop's mistress. I would be God's scarlet woman.

I used to take a shower at night, because it was so hot, and lie down naked on the cool marble floor so that the marble could inspire me with visions of weddings in *A Thousand and One Nights*.

Mama used to take me shopping on streets that ran perpendicular to rue Catinat to have little shantung and tussah dresses made for me, to buy me a

tortoise-shell bracelet, a green-jade pendant, a pair of
lizard shoes, in short, all the badges of little colonial girls.

We were always greeted by a Thi Nam who
would smile with all her black teeth showing.

"How much she looks like you."

"You'd think it had been made for her."

"She's the very image of her mother."

"It will bring you good luck. . . ."

"She looks exactly like you."

These Thi Nams frightened me a lot. I was convinced that it was always the same one who was
everywhere at once only Mama didn't know it, and
that this must be the yellow peril they talked about
on rue de Marignan. But once again, I had to keep
quiet. If I told that to anyone, I would be lost. . . .

The same Thi Nam served us mango sherbet at
La Pagode, the famous pastry shop on rue Catinat.
At home she was Nam, the *bep*'s wife, and it was
she who served me coffee under the mosquito net,
before I left for school. During the day she
frightened me less, but at night I trembled. . . .

School . . . it was called Chasseloup-Laubat and
was a hundred yards from the swimming pool. The
war was going on. We used to tell the concierge that
we had to go to defense practice and then we'd go

swimming. Sometimes (Saigon was a village) we'd order up a little party from the shops on rue Catinat and have it delivered to one of our professors: flowers, drinks, glazed pork, sweets (the nicest, the loneliest of them was Monsieur David). All he had to do then was invite his friends over. And the next morning we would see them reeling gaily along the trenches dug in the playground.

It was coeducational (the school). I can remember how fast—I was gifted but lazy—I would drop one course for another, Greek for no Greek, German which I didn't know for English which I did. I blocked on mathematics, rejected history, paid no attention to geography, and sneaked out of gym class; but I dreamed all day about the boys in the upper grades.

I was madly in love with a very dumb boy named Jean Arnal who had eyes like blue saucers. I was already hopelessly stuck on blue eyes: pieces of sky, I said to myself, and slipped him notes during recess. I wanted to take care of him. His mother had remarried. She did not love him. I clearly bored him with my attentions. He didn't know what to do with a little girl in heat who wanted to fondle him under false pretenses and had only the word "purity" on her lips. That was my way of being able to stand not being attractive: thinking of myself as pure, but it was also the seduction of Catholicism, the family, virtue, integration.

Ignorant little daughter of colonists, I wanted to be colonized.

But it was love I was most seriously involved with, desperately latching onto boys I hypocritically called my brothers.

That idea of brother meant everything to me. The family, the end of the unfairness of my fate as an only child, and man: man who smelled like good hot sand. Already the whole liturgy of odors and I mused about the last phrase of the *Paludes:* "The conquering captains have a strong smell."

My misfortune was that in my thirst for salvation I had fallen among Boy Scouts who, alas, respected me, primarily because Scouts respect others, but also because I still went around looking like a little Jewish girl in need of redemption, salvation, uplifting. I was gawky and flat-chested. In short, I had a lot to be worried about.

In 1938, a year before I arrived in Saigon, a Scout leader, Jean Rocher, idol of all the younger boys because of his good looks, intelligence, zeal, authority, and chastity had been found dead, naked, in his automobile, thirty kilometers from Saigon, in a forest of rubber trees. I can no longer remember the details, but he must have died in a Lawrencien struggle with himself or something like that.

Everyone talked about the boy. He was a legendary Catholic, a flawless Christian as transparent as mystic parchments. After his death, everyone had felt lost or had gone astray, especially another very handsome boy named Vincent Léry, son of a notary, a mixture of sheriff and bum, who flaunted himself at the Country Club swimming pool in Saigon with a beautiful Swedish blonde, a sort of incarnation of sin.

Since Jean Rocher's death, Vincent Léry no longer scouted, no longer worked in school, no longer went to mass, and gave every appearance of suffering a great moral decline.

I took it into my head to save him too. He was my only dark-eyed idol, and wallowing hypocritically in my salvationist drivel I decided to conquer him by subtly making use of Jean Rocher.

I learned as much as possible about him and about my future prey. I went busily from the old papa notary, to whom I paid strange visits on rue Pellerin during the siesta, to the brother and sister-in-law of the boy who had died as naked as a jay bird in a forest of rubber trees.

Perhaps he had died of love, I said to myself. Can you die of love cheating on God?

The Rochers were a childless Catholic couple. They were about forty and had very modest names: Paul and Jeanne. They were very Christian, very nice, but there was something withered about them. Withering is one of the signs of a lack of carnal zest for life.

People who have a sense of sin, a taste for sin, are withered also, but their withering is different: it is more authentic. It has the wrinkles of life, the stigmata of love.

During the siesta, I went out on my bicycle to have all my extrafamilial adventures. Saigon would be asleep, I would inhale the stifling odors of the heat, let go of the handle bars and make a wish as I rolled peacefully through the deserted city; then I would lean my bicycle against the garden fence of people-who-were-not-my-parents, push open a gate that was not our gate, looking like a little homeless prune (my grandmother used to call me her little prune), and I would get myself adopted by people who had nothing better to do. That, for me, was adventure.

I had already sensed that people understood the dead better than the living and, in my bid for emotional annexation, I got them to talk for hours about that extraordinary boy who had died mysteriously one October night, taking all his secrets with him.

I played the role of the unloved little girl without a family: my stepfather forbade me to convert until I reached eighteen. He was a wicked Freemason. There was a funny atmosphere at home. Something unhealthy, painful, bizarre. Mama was not motherly and my grandmother was dead. I was abandoned, rejected, lost, and hadn't He said, *Suffer little children to come unto me . . . ?* They were Christians! Let them open their garden gates so that I might sit among them in the shadow of the royal poincianas red as pepper, red as love, red as the blood of Christ, red as their liturgy. God was red. I would taste his body someday.

When I knew enough about that boy, that sterling Christian, dead perhaps of love in that forest, I summoned Vincent Léry to a vacant lot and told him, in utter seriousness, that Jean Rocher had appeared to me the night before and had asked me to take care of him, to save him from himself, to get him to read good books, to bring him back to God, and heaven knows what else.

I never quite knew what effect my Fatimesque

revelations had on him, but I did succeed, without his protesting too much, in integrating him into my network of brothers.

At home—under my white mosquito net— still waiting for that blood which never came— perhaps I would never be a woman—I dreamed. I dreamed that I was not my father's daughter but the daughter of the king of Poland. I began to resent my parents in earnest for having brought me into the world.

Where had I dredged up the king of Poland? From a book of Stories and Fables, I think, or *The Twelve Daughters of Queen Mab,* or because Poland had been invaded. I was within a few months of being the same age as the Princesses Elizabeth and Josephine-Charlotte, and I had been given a princess's education in Paris. But although black kings did exist there were no Jewish kings.

Why wasn't I one of the Dionne quintuplets? I dreamed of nothing but conventionalities, multiplicities, analogies. There were two testaments, three Graces, seven deadly sins, nine muses, and twelve apostles, but I remained irreparably alone and different.

How happy Dr. March's four daughters were,

how happy the Seven Dwarfs, and happy the thousand and one nights!

The feeling of not being like other people really pained me. I would have loved to have a twin sister who looked exactly like me, Christian, kneeling, pure, touched by grace. Grace was the only thing I wanted to have touch me. My brothers told me how other girls let themselves be had and I was scandalized. "Mademoiselles in name only," they said. This knowledge plunged me into the depths of despair, abysses which were illuminated only by the vision of the starving, hairless dogs that ran wild through a little street perpendicular to the house. It was a little street jammed with apartments, with narrow parallel houses squeezed up against each other where classmates less well-off than we lived. They were mostly from Martinique, Guadeloupe, or the West Indies and had names like Leblanc, Mondésir, or Renommée.

Confusedly, I had crossed racism off my list of prejudices, probably for self-serving and superficial reasons: my wish for personal integration and my desire to be Christian. But my revolt had already taken that direction and I probably would have advanced more quickly if Jesus had not been standing in my way.

I begged my stepfather to let me convert. "You have no right to stop me." He was an atheist at heart, though from a Catholic background, and forced us to eat steak on Good Friday (we ate fish almost every day in Saigon); that is my fondest memory of him, that pagan passion. He would answer that I didn't really know what I wanted yet and that I had to wait until I was eighteen.

Luckily, there was the Saigon Country Club, with its famous swimming pool where, entranced, I watched my brothers play water polo while purifying myself in the chlorinated water to which only whites or extremely distinguished half-breeds or quadroons were admitted.

There, as innocent as ever, I would dive between the boys' legs but would not dive between the girls'. Some tattletale told me that people were saying that I was a little tramp and that the Monnets, a very prolific, very Catholic family who went to mass every Sunday in that pink cathedral that was my most luminous vision, my blue line of the Vosges, my fairy-tale castle, had complained about me. There were six of them, and I can still see them marching along Indian file like six peas in a pod refusing to cast down their eyes upon the likes of me.

Actually, I was happiest diving between Matthieu's legs. He was a Scout leader, too, but still alive. Only he was engaged to Marie-Claude, the eldest of the peas-in-a-pod dynasty. These people, who were ardent Pétainists to boot, seemed to me, as I floundered in my morass of injustices, like the very symbols of virtue and happiness.

I also wrote long passionate letters to a naval officer, a devout Catholic too, who was stationed in Tourane. I must have been very unattractive, very worrisome, since everyone, men and women alike, seemed concerned only with my salvation and advised me to have a mysterious patience. I had no use for their patience, it was for His passion that I had been drawn to Christ and I rubbed up against the apostles the way one rubs up against one's partners at a country dance.

The first man to make a pass at me was a dermatologist my mother had sent me to because I had acne on my forehead. He looked at me from a little too close and then clasped me to him in a way that filled me with terror.

Those beautiful muscles I admired so much at the pool suddenly seemed positively fearsome and I plunged all the deeper into my devotions again.

There was a war going on, however, and the Japanese were everywhere. We hated them. Colonized Asiatics could still pass, but Orientals who colonized us—what a disgrace!

I still blush about the dance of joy we did in the streets of Cholon when we picked up leaflets, dropped from the sky, telling about Hiroshima.

The Japanese complained a lot about the French women who pretended not to see them. "How can it be, when French women are supposed to be so beautiful, so sensual, how can it be," the Japanese would ask, "how can it be that they have no facial expression?"

My stepfather listened to the British radio. I listened too but without understanding much. I contented myself with asking him if "it was good for us" and paid scant attention to his answer. All I thought about was understanding God and pleasing Him: I was a mystic flirt.

Burning, anguished letters from my grandfather came to us in Saigon. They were edged in black: he even had a mourning band for my grandmother on his writing paper, he who was so unfaithful to her, he who loved her so much. We would never see him again. My youngest uncle had been taken prisoner. We would never see him again either, and my uncle/my idol had left for London. He had left like a hero, catching a Czech boat just as it was sailing. A reserve officer, he had tossed his kepi and tunic into the water and shouted, "Vive la France anyhow!" climbing up a rope that had been thrown down to him. That made me feel better. My uncle/my idol would save France like Joan of Arc.

Having been brought up on rue de Marignan to worship my two uncles who had died for France, in a family where Patrie rhymed with *Chérie* and *Gloire* with *Victoire,* I stubbornly searched for something to rhyme with God. My grandfather also wrote us that anti-Semitism was spreading, but, bigot that I was, I didn't want to hear it.

My father's brother, who had died at twenty in 1918, had written a letter which had both soothed and troubled my childhood:

I am a member of a Jewish family which was naturalized French scarcely a century ago. My forebears, in accepting France's hospitality, became deeply indebted to her; thus I have a two-fold duty to perform, that of a Frenchman first, that of a new Frenchman second. This is why I feel that my place is where the risks are greatest.

. . . if I die I want my family to be able to point with pride to me so that never again will anyone be able to reproach them their foreign origins.

To deserve to be French, to deserve to be Christian, to deserve to be loved—more and more it seemed to me that Jews could only die, that life was denied them.

I desperately wanted to be tricolored and blond.

Opium

A STRANGE ODOR always wafted through our apartment on rue Garcerie, an odor of incense, jasmine, poppy, roses crushed with red peppers, caramel, and musty vestments.

I told this to a friend of mine, who answered, "But everyone in Saigon knows that your parents smoke opium."

That came as a terrible shock to me. Once again it had been proved that I would never be like other people.

So that was what the siestas were all about, the closed doors, the:

"You mustn't disturb him, he has a lot of work to do."

"But he promised to help me with my Latin translation."

"Later, darling."

"What are you going to be doing?"

"Keeping him company."

"But he has work to do."

"Exactly."

(And that was that.)

I started insulting them. People were dying in the war. We were occupied. France was being martyred. The Japanese were everywhere and they were smoking opium. With a great deal of patience they tried to explain to me that it was a harmless habit, that anyhow it was getting harder and harder to find any opium, that every intelligent person in Saigon smoked from time to time, first because there was nothing else to do and then because it was wartime.

I was indignant, revolted, scandalized. It was one more way of making me a social outcast.

Once again only God and his incense could make me forget that horrible smoke I had finally identified which was making slaves of them.

I would leave the odor of opium in the house for the odor of jasmine in the cathedral. *Lord have mercy upon me.* That was my favorite expression, along with the word "purity." If God had *mercy* upon me, I would be loved. In the Gospel it was written that one must love. I was quite willing to love everyone providing everyone loved me.

Voluptuously, I saw myself as a child-martyr, unloved, humiliated, while I martyrized my parents with my endless adolescence, my phony problems, my king of Poland who had abandoned me, France, also, which had vanished along with its seasons, the brothers I had never had, the grace we never said at table, the Convent of the Birds where I had not been allowed to be converted by Sister Jeanne-Marie whom my friend Chantal told me had an influence more troubling than love over all the young girls in Dalat. "You know," she said, "something utterly extraordinary happens when she calls you into her office to tell you you've done something bad. You feel so happy. So happy! You don't quite understand why she makes you lower your eyes and it feels like a kiss. You feel like snuggling up against her, like crying for hours. I love the sound of her skirts in the convent hallways. She makes me think of Catherine the Great, of Mary Stuart, of all the queens of heaven and earth. I love it when she's angry, especially when we're alone." I made up stupid voluptuous scenes in which I sobbed against her bosom, I who did not have one yet myself. . . .

Now I bless my opium-addict, Freemason step-father who denied me the Convent of the Birds. Between the Girl Scouts, where I was making a fool of myself—I had been placed in the Squirrel troop —and my cathedral, he thought that I was already engaged in enough holier-than-thou activities. Monster that he was, smoking opium, and in *my room*.

In fact, now that I knew, they no longer bothered to hide, and, separated from them by a curtain of wooden beads, I listened in horror as they turned into idiots:

World War Two won't bother you.
The only thing better than two Japs is one Jap. . . .

and they laughed stupidly.

"Guérin, you're really funny," raved a friend who was smoking with them.

Opium seemed to me to be the road to imbecility. I got back to the house as late as possible. I used to make detours on the way home from school: the cathedral, my Christian families, the hospital, the pastry shop, the botanical gardens where I went to read the Gospels.

"What are you doing here?"

"Nothing . . . I'm reading. . . ."

"What a funny thing to be reading!"

"What's so funny?"

"It's late, aren't your parents expecting you for dinner?"

"My parents never know what time it is."

"You poor kid!"

And in bed at night, before going to sleep, I would listen to their garbled tripe:

> You always need someone neater than you are.
> The Coromandel screen looks like a Corot.

It was a Sunday. On Sunday the whole world rejected me because I was not a Christian. On Sunday, I wept bitterly when people got up to take communion. There were "Mademoiselles in name only," adulteresses, bankers. Why not me?

I was walking down a path of scarlet royal poincianas, as scarlet as the Asia I rejected, breathing bougainvillaeas as purple as all the liturgy I dreamed about.

I hated Indochina, green and odorous. I hated exoticism. The Orient horrified me, I was born for the West with its falling leaves. Here the leaves never fell, they remained ruthlessly green. I hated lotuses, flowers resting like little Buddhas in the middle of lakes rimmed with pagodas, I hated the Antigones, the lamias, I hated the roots that choked the temples of Angkor and kept the Gods from breathing. I hated that sibylline people, I felt like a flag-waver, pompous and locked inside my moods. Blinded by the sun, I fled from what I later would passionately love for the rest of my life.

I hated the red earth, the banana trees, the rhododendrons. All I thought about was springtime budding, typically French smells, the days getting longer. I closed my heart to that supremely fertile vegetation for being alien and even the monkeys in the botanical gardens were my enemies. I did, however, pat the elephants with their rough, pathetic hides. I patted them without their being aware of it. An elephant's flank is like the Wailing Wall. Jeremiah—Bao-Dai—Ephraim—Norodom. I called to the Garden of Gethsemane to help me. After all, there had been palm trees in Bethlehem too.

We lived at the mercy of mosquitoes, and beside my bed, like incense, burned an incandescent little green snake: the *tortillon*. The *tortillon* lasted all night. It drugged the mosquitoes; it made them drunk.

At night, on the floor, like the light inside the tabernacle, the *tortillon*'s little ember protected me.

And in the stifling opiated night, I murmured, "May the Lord vouchsafe to bless this incense and receive it as pleasant perfume."

I addressed God with the familiar forms *tu* and *toi,* and tirelessly repeated, "Come, I beg of thee. Come unto me."

The smell of *nuoc mam* drifted over Saigon as it hung in the air above Phan Tiet. It rose up from the beaches like nausea. At Nha Trang, there were signs saying BEWARE OF SHARKS. My Corsican friends, army brats, were never afraid. One of them even got his left arm bitten off. They respected me too, but they taught me a few dirty words.

Nuoc mam was made of rotten fish, dried on the beaches, which, mixed with lemon and red pepper, became that astonishing sauce we put on rice. *Nuoc mam* was my Proustian little Madeleine, the counterpoint of opium, the smell from my childhood that I love. *Nuoc mam* was the reverse of the poppy and Tet was the opposite of Easter.

At Easter, there were church bells and eggs; at Tet, there were silk dresses, *nuoc mam,* pagodas, ginger and candied fruits and vegetables of all colors: lemons, turnips, grapefruits, and lotus seeds.

The rickshaw coolies, to get through their exhausting runs—and we shouted "Mao! Mao!" to make them run faster—smoked opium, too, and I can remember the soles of their feet, harder than buffalo horn, sticking out of the miserable stalls we glimpsed at the market.

The Saigon market. Noon. Siesta time. I didn't want to go home and breathe their incense. They wouldn't even notice me anyhow. Nam the boy would be preparing their little brown pellets that reeked of the caramel of malediction. "You're a good pipe boy. You come to France with us when the war is over."

I preferred munching on nougat in the market, sesame nougat. I stroked the pottery and gazed at the grains of rice in their transparent bowls. I had fun with my friends: we used to blow up the transparent little finger-shaped rubbers they sold in packs of six. We would fill them with cigarette smoke and make little balloons that floated off over our heads in the market. That made even the merchants laugh, but I didn't have the faintest idea that the little balloons were contraceptives. In Benares, a few years later, I wanted to buy rubbers of all sizes and colors, to give to my friends. The soldiers I was with seemed quite puzzled.

Before going back to school, my friends and I would gulp down a Chinese soup that burned our tongues and then drink coffee with crushed ice in it.

The street vendor would move away, banging his two sticks of wood against each other. I held the world at the end of my chopsticks.

All my life I have had a blinding nostalgia for the crushing heat of the siesta, when I never looked for shade like the opium addicts and rickshaw coolies.

Besides, it was in the market that I would see him, *him,* my opium addict/my love. He never saw me. I used to wonder where he was going, crouched in his rickshaw, at high noon. I wondered, but I also had a pretty good idea.

My first love looked a little like Christ without the beard. He was very thin, wasted by opium. He seemed to be on mysterious errands to me, when all the while he was only going from one den to the next. Whenever he had the desire or the need to smoke, he would stare straight ahead, expressionless. His rickshaw coolie would pedal, glistening with sweat, but he would not see me staring at him, ecstatic and aching, wondering how it would really feel to have a man take me in his arms.

I loved him passionately—the way one loves before knowing what love is. What is love? Do we invent love? Do we invent loving? What we do not invent is the suffering which comes to us from the other person. We are on the brink of the inexpressible. Happiness has always seemed to me like something that is about to be snatched away. This perhaps is why I have always had such an intense appreciation for moments of happiness, such a passion for the instant.

From that opium addict who would flee from me to his den, from the homosexuals I have truly loved and who could not love me, I have learned the meaning of the dispossession, the nonpossession of the other person. This knowledge has made me modest and combative. Everything that has been denied me has made me love life all the more.

Love has a thousand faces, among them the face of the person who rejects you. That dizzying moment when the earth gives way because the other person is there, because the other person is looking at you, because he seems to see you, that moment cannot be made to happen. It is because love transcends you that suddenly you are face to face with it and lower your eyes.

Oh, how I loved to lower my eyes when I was a girl, how I loved the confusion, how I loved the idea of love before I knew love! Is the world they hide from you more beautiful than the person who rejects you? I would have sold my soul for a real look from someone. When I feel very alone, I sometimes play at attracting looks, sometimes even in passing *métros* that are headed for distant stations, because there's no risk involved, and also probably because getting out from under a look can be terrible.

I have a friend who has a staggering look. All doubts and all despairs lie in her eyes, also utter sensuality and every passion; there is distrust, tenderness, and, perhaps most deeply, there is outrage. There is a light which comes from within. Sometimes there is a heart-rending clarity in black eyes, but my opium addict's eyes had no expression.

I do not know whether opium dilates or contracts the pupils, but I never saw myself in his eyes.

However, it was he, an opium addict, my parents' friend, my first love, who, between puffs of opium and attacks of malaria, taught me to read. He was very thin. His long hands, gaunt and yellowed as the first autumn leaves, hung down beside the rickshaw as I pedaled along beside him on my bicycle, dying of love, on the road to Gia Dinh.

It was during the war, the blackouts. He made me believe that he was in the Resistance and I rode beside him, accompanying him from one opium den to the next, when he wasn't smoking with my parents.

When he was, knowing nothing about the senses nor of how they could be deadened, I would be jealous of my mother, convinced that she was his lover. And yet he loved me. He loved the awkward little fourteen-year-old girl that I was. He had written to me: "I would give up opium for you like a pair of worn-out sandals," but I hadn't believed him. I had been afraid. I always had that acrid sweet smell in my throat that had poisoned my childhood and I refused to believe him. It seems that he married someone else eventually and got fat.

He gave me two years to make up my mind: two years to detoxify himself. He wrote me long, rambling letters every week. He spoke about our future children and wanted me to correct the mistakes in his letters so that they wouldn't laugh at him when they read them later. We were playing at posterity. But opium was stronger than the love he thought he felt for me. It was I who said no, but he was the one who was afraid.

When he came to the house, he always brought me books. It was he who made me move up from Delly and Henry Bordeaux, whose books I used to borrow feverishly from the Saigon Library in the hope of finding the keys to love in them, to real literature. I owe him that passion and also the ineffa-

ble discovery of the possibility of suffering for someone else. Tense, nervous, needing to smoke, his
gestures would get more and more jerky in his anxi-
ety to go and join my parents in the next room and
sink into drugged inanities with them, he who was
opening up the world for me. And I would watch.

When he left I would already be asleep. Naked
under my mosquito net, wrapped in my sheet, I
would have read the books he had just brought, I
would have read scowling, determined to insult him
when he went through my room on his way out, but
I always would have fallen asleep first, not without
having gone and glared balefully at the three of
them lying on the floor, one arm raised to allow the
opium to enter their lungs. I watched them—that
gesture was like an abominable salute to oblivion
for me—without their seeing me, lost in their idi-
otic dreams, lighting those little brown pellets for
each other that reeked of all the dreams I rejected
forever.

Drunk with jealousy, I would contemplate him
as he lay beside my mother like a living corpse, he
who dared say to me, "I cherish the dream of marry-
ing you." He cherished his dream but he never
touched me, all because of that curtain of brown pellets, that wall of smoke that rose between us.

When I wasn't idolizing him, I hated him. He worked for a press agency whose offices were on rue Catinat. When school let out, I raced down rue Catinat on my bicycle to catch a glimpse of him before going home to do my homework. If I didn't see him, I knew he was lying about in one of the numerous dens in the neighborhood.

Life was broadening. I had God and books between the world and me. My opium addict sneaked Renan and Huysmans onto my reading list, but nothing could shake my faith. I was a cathedral. I might be devoured by lions but I would die a Christian, redeemed, saved from all the terrible fates I dreamed up for myself. I would be a mother with amphoral hips from bearing nine children whom I would take to mass on Sunday, on my husband's arm. My sons would all go to the best schools but they would also know how to climb trees, my eldest daughter would become a nun and we would give her joyfully to God. Only the twins would stay behind in the colonies because France would need us. We would create the work of the flesh like a work of art. There would be bells and trumpets at our wedding. I would be ravishing in my organdy dress which would be transparent only to him. Everyone would say, "How beautiful she is, how pure." I would wear two pearls in my ears like dewdrops, pearls as transparent as my soul.

I had found a new family for myself, Catholic of course, and very prolific: the Renans. And I loved this family almost gaily. The wife had said to me one day—her name was Juliette—"Whenever he touches me, I lose all track of what I'm doing." I understood that this was the explanation for that large family and perhaps also a definition of love.

I was happy to take care of their children at night. Any other house seemed sweeter than my own. That was the first time I ever heard the water being turned on at night, several times during the night. I might dream about baptismal water, but I realized that there were other wellsprings. . . .

With the Renans and some other people we organized an acting company and for a few days I managed to tear my opium addict away from his little pellets.

We put on Cocteau's *Oedipus Rex*. He played Oedipus. I was in the chorus with three other girls.

> "We know that you are not a god.
> But the only mortal able to save us.
> Help us.
> Your glory is at stake."

Jocasta was an army officer's daughter and Creon
the son of the director of the Shell company. He was
another one of my brothers, but he played golf and
tennis while we splashed around in our beloved
swimming pool. He was very witty and told me
risqué stories that entranced me, fool that I was.
Thanks to him, I had his mother's bosom to cry on,
and she gave me her old dresses, since Mama, lost
in her wild fogs, no longer bought me little shantung blouses. I adored having her to feel sorry for
me. I had gone up one notch in the litany.

They had the most beautiful villa in Saigon, but
their wealth did not shock me. I told myself that I
might well become the very genteel, very Catholic
wife of a company director someday, if he loved me.
Was worldy power inccompatible with my faith?
No, since I would give him everything. I would offer
him my life in exchange for that power. Our water
noises then would be luminous, phosphorescent
fountains. When I got home from the palace the
Laurens (they were the Shell company director's
family) lived in, our two rooms looked like a garret;
their garden was fragrant with frangipani while our
place smelled of the incense that leads souls to hell.

I played queens, by myself, at night. A lawn
against a rice paddy. The Holy Mother against my

mother. A Christian family against a Jewish family. I invented an insane barter system to get myself into the ranks of the elect.

The war was moving backward, it seemed. Prisoners from Sumatra, Java, and Bali were being held in the outskirts of Saigon, behind barbed-wire fences.

At siesta time, riding around on our bicycles, we came upon some gorgeous blue-eyed boys being guarded by the Japanese.

The first day we just gave them a big smile, but then visiting them quickly became ritual. We tried to give them the news—which was good—by singing mysterious songs at the top of our lungs which the Japanese couldn't understand at all. The Corsican boys, army brats, had given us the idea. They used to sing out, in Corsican dialect, the translation of the Latin exam under the windows of the Chasseloup-Laubat grammar school. Unfortunately, they had got caught because they had sung one phrase which the Machiavellian headmaster had purposely left out.

We were caught ourselves, through our own carelessness, along with a friend from Martinique, a Boy Scout of course, because we greeted the prisoners with a V-for-victory sign. The Japanese beat us. They insulted us, spat in our faces, said that we were losing the war, and pounded us to a pulp (especially my black friend). However, we were released that same night, thanks to the intervention of a friend of my friend the opium addict who brought a Scout manual to the Japanese to prove that the V we had made was only the Scout salute.

I was a heroine by breed and worthy of my uncle/my idol who fought for us in England. I exaggerated that story until, according to me, we had even been tortured. After the liberation, the Americans gave me a chance to identify my tormentors. For the first time I looked a Japanese in the eye: he was the one who had spat in my face. He lowered his gaze. I said that I couldn't identify him *positively*, thereby saving Susuki from the firing squad. He looked at me, overwhelmed (I forgot that the Japanese had no expression in their eyes).

In all good faith, I invented lies that corresponded to the way I imagined my life, my story, my biography to be. I was ridiculously touched by them but, above all else, I hoped that they would touch others.

I had a special propensity for stories about apparitions.

When I was a little girl, Queen Astrid had appeared to me after that marvelous vacation in Knokke-Le Zoute, with her ghost of a smile, and had asked me to take care of King Leopold. But I was very young then, only eleven years old. She had just died in a horrible automobile accident, bent over the road map, beside the king, her husband. They had loved each other as much as on the day they had first met. Everything predestined me to take care of the king: they had been married the same year I was born and she had died the year of my own parents' remarriage. But the burden of responsibility for the king frightened me and I begged my beloved queen to ask him to wait a few years.

Stories about apparitions were my favorites. Three seas separated me from France, so I could lie to Mama and, still in my religious vein, I told her about the visit I had paid to my uncle Bergson, which was true, boulevard Beauséjour, which was true also. Why had they taken me there? Perhaps because my grandmother had just died, perhaps because Jeanne, her daughter, our deaf-mute cousin, had wanted to get to know me.

In any case, I had read about his conversion to Catholicism in the newspapers and I told Mama that, when I was with him, alone in his office, as if he could guess what was going on inside me, he had pointed to a crucifix above his head.

Had I seen the crucifix or had it been in the news-paper? That Bergson should make such a gesture to a great-grandniece whom he did not know and who still was obediently attending religious instruction classes at the synagogue on rue Copernic seems highly suspect to me. But that is the story I told Mama about that meeting.

I had another apparition story, this one more modest, about Charles Trenet appearing at a Girl Scout meeting. I had written to him, he had adored my letter, he had come, he had sung for us, he had patted my cheek as he left and said, "You're a mar-velous little girl."

Mama had been quite struck. Charles Trenet!

We played his records over and over again, tire-lessly. They were all we had left of France: *Quand notre cœur fait boum, Mam'selle Clio, Mam'selle Clio.* Her little girl was marvelous!

Luckily, communications with France were cut and Mama, who seemed vague in other respects, could check up on neither Bergson nor Trenet.

So I had the two of them safely to myself as long as the war lasted.

As for the apparition of that mysterious young man, that took place in Saigon in a vacant lot and the only person I ever talked to about it was Vincent Léry, who certainly never mentioned it to anyone else.

Had Jean Rocher been in love with him? I wonder about it still. *Whoso privily slandereth his neighbor, him will I cut off!* There was a whole series of little phrases from the Bible that seemed to me to be the keys to the world. I mixed them up with a few phrases from Claudel and Peguy, and —on good days—from Gide. *For I can tell you truthfully, Nathanael, each desire has enriched me more than the always false possession of the object of my desire.*

The Gospels for me were the gates to love. I found in them all the contradictions, all the follies, all the instincts I dreamed about, between the lines, without realizing it.

And yet, neither the healings of the sick, nor of the possessed, nor the resurrections of the dead really dazzled me.

What I did discover was that Jesus loved the lazy, the poor, the prodigal sons, the women of easy virtue, that the kingdom of heaven was not for the brains, and that the lost sheep was the favorite.

Consider the lilies how they grow: they toil not, they spin not; and yet I say unto you, that Solomon in all his glory was not arrayed like one of these.

God gave out a sweet smell. God was there and the Word was made flesh and it lived among us. Mary Magdalene was my favorite. Hidden inside me as I still wallowed complacently in virtue—in the sly hope of finding myself in a stable between an ox and an ass, the second Mother of God—hidden and yet luminous was the fact that already all I loved in that religion was the flesh that it denied.

My stepfather was mobilized in Luang Prabang. I knew that he still smoked opium in his khaki uniform. And what if we lost the war because of him? I had to do something to exorcise that smoke, to save France, my country, our flag: I always had a mystical suit of armor inside my head.

I ran to the hospital. I volunteered, offered myself, gave myself. They accepted me. I became a nurse's aide. Redemption, I held you close to my heart. They dressed me in white. I washed the wounded in the morning. I washed their faces— how sweet was their stubbly skin—I caressed the Savior's thorns, I shaved them, I washed their feet and held the basin like holy water while they brushed their teeth. Then Sister Bernardine came along behind me and washed the soldiers' unmentionables (what were they called: members, organs, sexes?). She said, "That's no job for you."

We had to move once again into an even smaller apartment on boulevard Norodom, right near my beloved pink cathedral which I learned had been brought stone by stone from Marseille. We built cathedrals with our pink stones while beneath their baobabs the temples of Angkor still stood, their stones ravaged by the sun. Those moves into smaller and smaller apartments were the only real consequences of the war for us, all the beautiful houses having been requisitioned for the last glorious days of the wicked Japanese.

It was the first Viet attack on Saigon before the Liberation, an ambiguous period during which the Japanese made a pretense of collaborating with the Vietnamese before their ultimate defeat. It was siesta time at home. For once I was not out on my bicycle because I had to review for the final exams which were approaching as rapidly as the end of the war. A group of Vietnamese had occupied the building. All the white men were bound hand and foot. My stepfather and a few friends were smoking their daily little pellets behind a screen. Again there was a strong odor of opium in the room and two men were groveling and moaning. I was ashamed. They were groveling for their pellets. But who were these Vietnamese who had come to tie them up? I raced down the stairs. Among them I recognized one of my Scout-leader friends, Ton. I asked, very arrogantly, "What's got into you? You've gone crazy. . . ." He spat in my face and said, "Someday, you'll understand. . . ."

That spit was my real baptism but it took me years to understand this. That Vietnamese boy named Ton, that Vietnamese boy who is no doubt dead today, or still fighting in the rice paddies, that Vietnamese boy who spat in my face, he made me understand what I was incapable of understanding all by myself and which I was not likely to find in Mallet and Isaac.

I was not a racist and I hated the Vietnamese only because they were the best students in my class. Lazy myself, I loved dunces of all colors. Leblanc and Renommée (two West Indians) and Alexandre and myself (two whites), all liked each other a lot because we often were ranked thirty-fourth (out of thirty-four). I thought that this was what equality was all about. And yet the first time I saw a wounded Vietnamese on the sidewalk in Saigon, I was astonished that his blood was red like ours.

Opium was starting to get scarce. It was part of a Japanese ploy to subjugate the addicts. My stepfather, very agitated, could get only dross to smoke, the residue. On certain days he was limp as a rag, imploring us to find him some real opium. On those days, my contempt knew no bounds. Once or twice, we had to take him to a clinic to be detoxified. Then, I really lived my martyrdom to the hilt. *Nothing will be spared me, My God, I am not worthy, Give me the grace to, Grant me, Remission, Salvation, Light.* There were not enough sweet words to purify this "fall" which I took as a threat to my possibilities for salvation.

I used this as an excuse to let my schoolwork slide, surrendering myself to my devotions, my sorrows and tears. Only Nam, the boy, was not fooled. He would say to me, "If Mademoiselle no give a damn like that, me no give a damn either, Mademoiselle flunk her exams and Mademoiselle ruined for life."

I let him talk. There were only a few more months to wait. I had two spiritual advisers, Dom Bernard, a fascinating Jesuit who was supposed to baptize me in Dalat, and Father Morel, a very nice man, our Scout chaplain, who went swimming with us, at Cap Saint-Jacques, his beard bobbing like a little boat out in front of him.

I licked the sea salt off my arms at Cap Saint-Jacques. I licked it, flattened against the burning sand.

I was at the end of the wilderness, at last, and the salt I awaited was the salt of the earth.

There was nothing left that I could do for the little light of the tabernacle, to exorcise the sickly flame of the oil lamp that always burned in my parents' bedroom.

Baptism

I WOULD GO to my beloved cathedral and watch weddings celebrated by Father Moulard, famous for all the children with which he had peopled Cochin-China and for the rascalities of his confessions, which I would later verify. He always asked, my little friends explained to me, if you'd done things you'd never even thought of doing.

Father Morel, after drying his beard, had written this message for me on a picture of the Holy Virgin: "May She finally grant you the so greatly desired joy of your rebirth."

He had found the one word that could bring tears to my eyes. God could offer me only one thing: a second birth, but would it not be more difficult for a

87

little Jewish girl to enter the Church than for a camel to pass through the eye of a needle?

From being fourteen, I finally got to be eighteen years old and "the so greatly desired joy of your re-birth" was at hand.

Dom Bernard was to baptize me in Dalat. I had a very Catholic doctor for a godfather. The widower of a beautiful Corsican, he was a Corsican himself, and photos of his young wife (what is more radiant than a dead young woman?) lighted up every room in his house. He had two daughters and to help bring them up was going to marry my godmother.

I had once again constructed a fake Catholic family that accepted me as a little lost sheep wounded by my wicked parents, and the fear of hell seemed like a delight in comparison. Never again would I be tortured by flames other than the Holy Ghost's little tongues of fire! In one fell swoop I was going to get all three of them: The Father, the Son, and the Holy Ghost.

Finally the time had come. Four years of suffering and now Jesus in my arms. I was in a depraved sort of ecstasy.

Of course all my brothers were at the church. For the first time in my life I would be able to go up behind them and eat the Host. Finally, I would be like everyone else, and my joy equaled my martyrdom.

I no longer remember whether there was music, but if there were flowers they were white. The air was sweet and Dom Bernard made an unctuous and patronizing little speech entrusting me with the weapon that would protect me from everything forever: prayer.

When I stuck out my tongue to take communion, I was suddenly filled with emptiness, and knew that the whole thing was a disaster. God was not there. He never would be there. I had taken the wrong road, God did not exist, my "brothers" were dupes, the Blessed Virgin would never be my mother: my mother was Mama whom I had rejected. I was a mortal offense to those who had tried, against their will, to save me. I understood all this in a flash but, like the case of the Thi Nam with black teeth whom I thought was always the same person, I knew that I must tell no one, if only because my stepfather would have gloated so hatefully between puffs of dross.

The body of our Lord was a fraud. A substitute for everything that I would really love in life.

My marriage was a failure. Like my mother, I would have to get divorced but I mustn't tell them that right away. They would be too smug.

I would keep going through the gestures of love as I looked for love. If love did not come, there would be time enough to deal with that. For once I was going to keep quiet. Even during confession.

To lie about love. What a ball! I was learning about adultery before my wedding night.

So I returned each day, unmoved, stupefied, to that pink cathedral where I had worn my knees out praying for acceptance.

The red velvet seemed shabby to me, the wood no longer smelled sweet, the incense had gone sour. I had the sensation that the red carpet that led to the altar had been pulled out from under my feet. It suddenly had become as mundane as the green rug in the casino where my grandfather placed his cursed bets. I had fallen flat on my face on that rug and the Host had tasted stale. And yet I had swallowed it. And the blood of Christ had not choked me either, diaphanous tubercular that I dreamed of being.

Oh, if only the Host had been like cayenne pepper, like paprika, or red pepper! Oh, if only the Host were fiery as they claimed! But no, it was bland,

and I no more knew what to do with their blandness than they knew what to do with my tempers.

I became as aggressive with God as a woman who has finally landed a husband. I secretly tried to place the blame on my stepfather: if he hadn't made me wait so long, God would have desired me more. I had been betrayed by words which were like sedan chairs, mystical palanquins that should carry us dancing above the crowd. Betrayed by ecstasy, betrayed by intoxication, betrayed by rapture: God had stood me up.

The bread and wine were not made for those rice-paddy countries and I was not made to sit at their table.

I learned about confession and lying simultaneously. I was interesting, wounded, duped, a tease perhaps.

What was religion?

What was love?

I saw it on the features of every Virgin in the world (Holy Virgin) offering one full breast to her newborn son and saving the other for her beloved husband.

A sublime sharing.

Your son, a lark.

Your daughter, a partridge.
Your husband: roses.
Desire: a forest, the sea, beaches, seasons.

They took insane risks in the Garden of Eden.
Man lived there peacefully, with nothing to do, fondling his missing rib, completely naked, and already, by the eighth day of creation, there were portents of death.
  —*Who revealed to you that you were naked?*
  —*The woman you put with me offered me that fruit and I ate.*
The first man, a stool pigeon?

Fortunately for me, my mystical defeat coincided, within a few months, with the actual liberation of Indochina.

In August 1945, British troops entered Saigon. It was a spectacular time.

These British were Hindus. I owe them everything.

To the third wise man, to Balthasar, to black kings, I owe the heavens which suddenly opened for me.

India

THE LIBERATION was a celebration we had not deserved, my parents because of their drugs and I because of God.

But the Hindus had not come to reproach us for this: they had their own problems. As Her Britannic Majesty's subjects they had come to liberate the whites and they were supposed to fire on the yellows. They drank at night to forget.

There had been a few collaborators in Indochina. We had not been among them. Our opium stupor and genuine republican sentiments. Also the fact that because of the drug my parents had not been assimilated and thus had been saved from the "National Revolution."

97

I made friends with three Hindu officers. I do not think that colonial young ladies would have been allowed to go out with common soldiers, for on that subject our pseudo-liberal education was serenely reactionary. I was still barricaded inside my virtue, confusing virginity with the notion of a gift which emanated from my prayer books. I still complained about my family life, my loneliness, the smell of opium that hung heavily in the house, and the general incomprehension of which I was the object.

They made me see the real poverty, not the one I persisted in not seeing in Indochina, not the nice clean beggars in the Gospel, but the world's poverty, the injustice that comes not only from the barrenness of the soil but also from the System. They did this with the extraordinary tact of people who refuse to be pitied because that might be too much for them to bear.

They also taught me to laugh. I remember jeep rides—after the curfew—with these handsome soldiers. The youngest of them was a medic whom we called the Kid Doctor. He was very proud of his mustache, which he stroked all the time the way girls run their hands through their hair.

I had moved imperceptibly from holy water to rice wine, from war to peace, and from the Apostles to the army.

One star-filled night—why, I wondered, was the sky the same everywhere and not the earth?— we convinced the Kid Doctor that he had lost his mustache in the grass. Drunk with freedom, on all fours in a forbidden garden, we searched for hours with a tiny flashlight for the mustache. The Kid Doctor, meanwhile, believed he was as naked as the Emperor in the Andersen fairy tale.

The Hindus organized parties at night in Gia Dinh where I used to bicycle with my opium addict during the Japanese occupation. They lit bonfires. Bonfires because the war was over when the war was just beginning. The Sikhs and Gurkhas danced war dances to celebrate the peace while I, stupid as usual, could only dream of getting back to my promised land "France" with her flag, her four seasons, her Champs-Élysées, her snow and her dead leaves. I dreamed of a cozy temperate climate.

In Saigon there was a little four-year-old girl who had swallowed a coffee bean that had lodged in her lung. My father had just sent me an airplane ticket that would allow me to get back to France. I offered to take the little girl with me to have her treated in Calcutta. Her parents, who had five other children, couldn't have left Saigon for several weeks. The trip could have been dangerous for the little girl but as I was still a minor they didn't want to issue me a certificate releasing me from responsibility.

Since the ways of the Lord are impenetrable, she coughed up the coffee bean before boarding the plane.

So I arrived in Calcutta with just a few addresses in my pocket, among them that of the parents of a Bengali friend, Subrata, handsome as the sun, a Communist, newly married, who wanted me to stay at his house in India so that I could find myself, fake lost little girl that I was.

I spent the most beautiful month of my life with his parents at 37 Ekdalia Road, in Calcutta, in a family overflowing with all the love I thought I had been deprived of—that was still in the period when I was rejecting my mother—wishing I had been orphaned forever the day my transparent grandmother with the pale water-green eyes had died.

Subrata's father taught Shakespeare in a Calcutta high school. He was a kindly and silent man. When I left, he said, "You brought some sunshine into my life." My cousin pointed out to me that in India perhaps that was not a compliment.

I left their house the day I discovered that they had given me their only room and were sleeping on the floor in the front hall, where I had learned to eat chapattys and little balls of yoghurt and banana with my fingers. They had given me their bed. In India, you really give everything you have.

I left them, but I never really left them. I learned Bengali at the School of Oriental Languages just to be able to tell myself that someday I would once again race back up their stairs and they would say, "She's come back."

Twenty-five years have passed but the desire to rush into their arms remains unchanged. Today Subrata's father is dead. They have moved but I know that I will climb another flights of stairs to see his widow, our mother, and that she will clasp me in her arms and say, "My child."

I spent a few days in Benares, where I saw the sacred cows, the steps that go down to the Ganges, and a widow being cremated on her pyre. It was not the timeless poverty that was the most awful, it was the feeling that it would never end. Resolving India's poverty would be like emptying the ocean with a thimble.

I saw a little English boy in a restaurant, cherubic, ravishing, curly-headed, in a light, freshly laundered sailor suit, holding out a crust of bread behind a window to an emaciated little beggar boy.

The same day I saw a little girl carrying a starving child on her hip. He vomited. She ate what he had just vomited.

Then I returned to Calcutta and the day I got there, after a demonstration, the English police fired on some students, killing nineteen of them. The son of a neighbor of the Banerjees', the friends I was staying with, was killed. The police who had just fired on those students were the same as the police who allowed me to walk safely through the streets of Saigon.

Blinded by my own problems, I had been incapable of understanding injustice as a thing in itself.

I tried to find an answer to the inequality by wearing saris. This disguise solved nothing, but I did make friends who taught me what I was unable to learn on my own. By dint of trying to find myself, I had found others. My heart pounded each time I went to meet them.

My life is an immense debt to other people, for I have never acquired anything on my own. Nothing. I was going to say perhaps my mannerisms. But no, other people have taught me everything. I have learned to unlearn things but I have not made any discoveries. I learned everything as I made my way toward other people, and when sometimes I feel like being alone, it is in order to know them better when we meet again.

And it was this path that led me to writing. It was a way of shyly soliciting affection. I wrote to say that I loved but then I also wrote to be loved.

In Calcutta, in the Chowringhee section, I saw people sleeping in the street. Like children. Ecstatic, mystical, foolish, I said to Subrata's father, "How beautiful this country is, where people sleep in the street, where the sun . . ."
Subrata's father answered, "Child, they are not sleeping, they have died of hunger."

The next morning, I took the first tramway and saw the street cleaners picking up the sleepers. They picked them up without the slightest trace of emotion. It was not their indifference that struck me, it was the ordinariness: those corpses were like our parking violations.

I went into the churches of Calcutta to seek the answer. The black priests smiled like bank tellers behind their windows. Men who knew that they possessed the sure truths: money, poverty, death.

France

WE, I AND MY little coffee-bean girl, landed in Paris in a Dakota after a stop in Cairo, a still English Cairo, which was, in a way, an answer to my childhood dreams about the Pyramids.

Jewish-Egyptian merchants described the war to me. It was the first time that I had heard anything about . . . But how could I darken the joy of the Liberation with that knowledge? It still seemed impossible to me.

I haggled over the price of a hideous red blouse in Khan-el-Khalili. I had found my people again, but I didn't want any part of them.

When we landed at Le Bourget airport, the little girl asked, "Is this Calcutta, or is this Cairo?"

It was Paris, it was autumn, the leaves were dead, it was cold, and there I was.

When I got back to France, I suddenly discovered all the things I hadn't known about, saccharin, barley coffee, ration stamps, restrictions, and the camps, and I was compelled to be a hypocrite.

Almost the entire Toulousian branch of the family had been deported. Aunt Jeanne gassed at Birkenau, the Molinas from Bordeaux, Élie with her sweet face whom I loved so much, Andrée who was unable to have children. The Zadoc Kahns, gentle as angels, dead in the train that was taking them to the camp, their son Bertrand, our doctor, preceding Thierry de Martel in his suicide the day the Germans entered Paris, Michel Bauer dead at Dachau, Serge and Liliane Meyer Oulif, whom I used to play with on Sundays, dead with their mother at Buchenwald.

I discovered the real Jewish Martydom instead of the one I had made up for myself. All those people had died simply because they were Jews, while I had been making such a fuss not to be one any more.

Every Wednesday, I lunched with my Uncle Alfred, my great-grandmother's brother from Toulouse, an old Cartesian scholar who was dismayed by my baptism. We ate *raie au beurre noir* which I hated and flan that trembled on my plate. He told me about the war, the Occupation, the yellow star. One day, on the *metro*, at the Picpus stop, a man had come up to him, looked at the star sewn onto the lapel of his jacket, and said, "Monsieur, I feel very sorry for you."

But things were also more complicated than that. My cousin Michel, who had joined the Resistance at fifteen, had been imprisoned in Drancy and narrowly escaped. His mother—my father's sister—converted to Catholicism out of gratitude. He also converted not at all out of opportunism but because the priest who hid them during the war had drawn them toward God without their being aware of it. My aunt's faith was fanatical, radiant, totalitarian and her happiness at thinking of me as a Christian was such that I remained a prisoner of my beads and prejudices for a few more months.

My great-grandmother, jolted by Hitler out of her wonderful life of family, cruises, and bridge, underwent the disgrace of the yellow star in the Basque country. Heartbroken by my grandmother's death, and perhaps also in order to dispossess my grandfather, she put all the family furniture in storage and moved into a hotel in Biarritz. In 1914, she had come from Épinal to live at the Majestic in Paris. That was the beginning of the end of our purely provincial lives. Her worst memory was of a night spent in a brothel in Pau during the exodus, in 1940.

All the Germans had had to do then was carry off the crates of signed antiques that my grandmother had lovingly selected from dealers in Épinal and Gérardmer. All that remained were the names of these pieces I used to hide behind as a little girl with my cousin Yves: one inlaid commode, one carved-wood Louis XV armchair, one black-and-gold lacquer screen.

She was outraged whenever she saw me leave to go and pray in the cathedral in Bayonne. I could not yet admit to her that I felt myself becoming more and more Jewish every day.

She was also shocked because Mama blew cigarette smoke out through her nose and because I walked around naked in my bedroom (those colonials!). When she took a taxi, she would forget that she hadn't had a chauffeur for over thirty years and say, without turning a hair, "Home, please." She called beggars "poor devils" and tipped the doorman at the casino in Biarritz five francs on the days she won at roulette. Even when gambling, she remained very "family," and although she played the zero and the last six numbers, she also played all our birth dates, which gave her winnings a tinge of morality. When I slipped the doorman a hundred francs behind her back, she would give me a rap with her umbrella and say, "You'll wind up in the poorhouse." She also told me, flouting my beads and missals, "You're going to marry a Jew." She knew what she was saying.

It happened a few years later. In Hirsingue, in 1950. My great-grandmother was radiant. Her husband had come from the neighboring village: Durmenach. The tribe was reunited. A progressive young rabbi married us. I was happy to be getting married.

We were married in the garden. Under a Jewish canopy, but it seemed gayer than that and we only partly had the feeling that we were making concessions.

The rabbi chatted with us before the ceremony. In passing, he asked if we had ever been converted. A flight of white doves rose above my head. For six

years I had swallowed that Host that had resisted
me. I said, "Why are you asking us that?" "Because
in that case, we'd have to baptize you again, im-
merse you in icy water." It was June twenty-seventh,
however. A brilliant sun. Bells. Storks. *Tête de veau
ravigote. Foie gras.* Gewürztraminer, champagne,
and schnapps, but I didn't want to catch cold for a
truth that was no longer mine. Since we were having a religious service to please our parents, I decided to lie, by omission.

Some homosexual friends were at our wedding.
The rabbi, after evoking the difficulties of a time
that had sunk from Voltairian skepticism to degen-
eracy before foundering in existentialism said to me,
"When people come to your house, my dear little
lady, they'll be able to say: '*How goodly and joyful
are thy tents, O Jacob.*'" Our angels smiled.

Six years later, we were divorced. My ex-husband
wanted to remarry in a synagogue. So I wrote to the
priest who had baptized me to ask him to send my
baptismal certificate. He couldn't get over it. There I
was still in the fold, his former little lost sheep. He
sent it to me with his fondest wishes. What he did
not know was that I was asking him for my baptismal certificate in order to be able to prove that our
religious marriage had been invalid, since I had
lied.

But before our Jewish wedding, there had been that long period of "religious dishonesty."

I had been torn apart by my family, my seasons, my inner anguish, my confusion, and my disarray.

It was at Sainte-Clotilde church—we lived on rue Casimir-Perier—that I tried in vain to pray. I knelt beside my aunt, who wrapped herself in a black mantilla and tried, dazzled by God, to cram me full of gospels and epistles and to persuade me that we were the elect, infatuatedly convinced that we possessed the truth. Surreptitiously, at her side, I read Baudelaire at Easter and Lautréamont for Pentecost.

As time passed, I felt myself becoming like the little old Jewish lady, who, having lost her keys, goes to Saint Anthony of Padua to ask him in Hebrew to find them for her.

I stumbled on rue du Pot-de-Fer. "Paris which is only Paris when she rips up her paving stones." I learned about the war from poems, because the people who could have talked to me about it were ashamed or dead.

Astounded, I discovered the gold of autumn, which one can kiss until mid-September in Saint-Innocents Square. I discovered postwar Paris, a Paris which lacked everything but was alive under its stony façades.

In Indochina, they had told us that the Germans had carried off the Eiffel Tower to melt it down into tanks and guns. How comforting to see it standing there, gray and transparent, on its grassy plot!

I tried to find in books what I was not yet able to find in life.

But I got everything backward. I felt myself to be unloved because of words too.

Even Baudelaire complicated my life. It was impossible to hear:

Even when she walks she looks as though she's dancing

How could I ever be like that? I was uncoordinated. I was even incapable of playing basketball in Saigon. I did not know how to dance. I would never know how to dance. I tossed and turned in my bed, darkly repeating:

One night as I lay beside a hideous Jewish girl,
As beside a corpse a laid-out corpse.

There was no way out for me. I sincerely believed this and, ready to fall into sin, having no sense of sin, I told myself that no one would ever want me except my opium addict who kept following me around distractedly, his worn pair of sandals in his hand.

The God of love had made a fool of me. I did not yet know that soon I would wrap myself in the satiny Scrolls of the Tables of the Law and finally become a Queen of the Sabbath.

It was a truly difficult period in which I would have to get myself banished for a betrayal which was no longer mine. I was crossing the Red Sea again, but against the tide.

I bought *Notre-Dame-des-Fleurs* and *The Miracle of the Rose* by Jean Genet, probably so as not to abandon my pink cathedral completely. I was stunned by the great beauty, but once again bewildered. What I remembered about Genet—to whom I would later owe everything—was that Bulkaen, the hero of *The Miracle of the Rose,* after making love to a woman, felt like breaking a bidet over her head.

I was still in a state of total confusion, and idiocy, but I knew that I was on the verge of seeing clearly. My imaginary hurts would not have been in vain. I was finally nearing the shore.

One day, I found myself by chance in the country, in Châteauroux, I think, and unable to bear it any longer, I decided to go and confess and for once to tell the truth.

The priest listened to me. He had a very young, very sympathetic voice. I told him *everything*. He said simply, "Do not stay a minute longer in this church where you have no business being and where you will only come to grief. You're on the wrong track. You weren't meant for the Catholic religion. It was not meant for you. Get out."

There I was, banished at last. What a miracle! I was crazy about the priest. I wanted to see him again at all costs. I wanted to marry him. I wanted to see him outside the confessional. I waited for him at the door of his church the way I used to wait for boys outside the Chasseloup-Laubat school, but he sent me back to my Jewish roses and the lilies of Israel and I had to catch my train for Paris.

God had finally jilted me. My mystical flirtation was over. I had been voluptuously repudiated. What I would keep from my pilgrimage through that pink cathedral would be Carpaccio and Mozart. And love.

I would make necklaces out of my rosary beads,

and sell myself for a cantata. Now I took the little jade bracelet and placed it at my temple. I was Jewish. I was pagan. And I was free.

Religion had been my drug. I had kicked the habit.